I'm a DRAGON

By Mallory C. Loehr
Illustrated by Joey Chou

For Phoenix van Rhyn, my dragon boy —M.C.L.

 A GOLDEN BOOK • NEW YORK

Text copyright © 2019 by Mallory C. Loehr.
Cover art and interior illustrations copyright © 2019 by Joey Chou.
All rights reserved. Published in the United States by Golden Books, an imprint of Random House
Children's Books, a division of Penguin Random House LLC, 1745 Broadway, New York, NY 10019.
Golden Books, A Golden Book, A Little Golden Book, the G colophon, and the distinctive gold
spine are registered trademarks of Penguin Random House LLC.
rhcbooks.com
Educators and librarians, for a variety of teaching tools, visit us at
RHTeachersLibrarians.com
Library of Congress Control Number: 2018942827
ISBN 978-1-9848-4944-1 (trade) — ISBN 978-1-9848-4945-8 (ebook)
Printed in the United States of America
10 9 8 7 6 5 4 3 2 1

I've got scales. . . .

I've got wings. . . .

I love precious things.

I'm a **DRAGON!**

I live in a cave.
Visit me if
you're brave. . . .

I'm not a liar—

I breathe
FIRE!

I can be loud.
Hissss.

I can be quiet.

Hmmmm.

I own the skies!

Wheeee!

My family lives
all over the world—

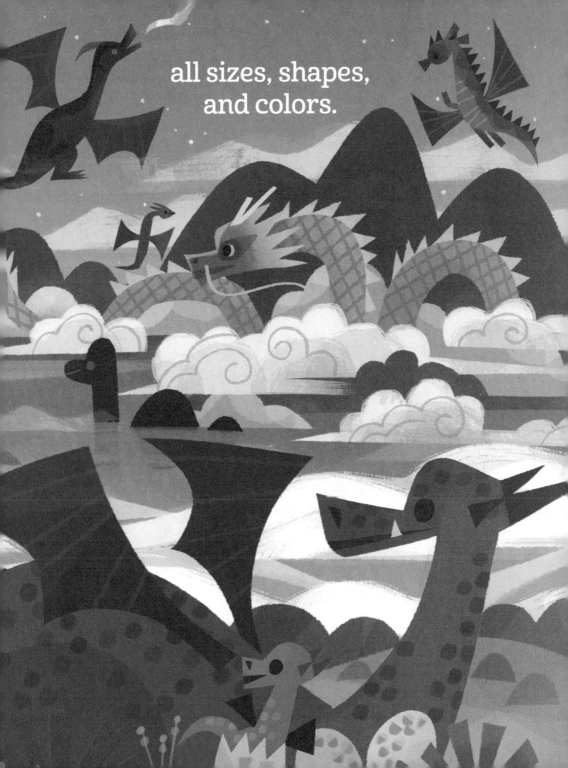

all sizes, shapes, and colors.

Some of us
can swim.

There are many kinds
of dragons!

I can get in a fight
to show my might.

I am dangerous.

I am delightful.
I am different.